I, Bruno

ORCA
Echoes

I, BRuNo

CAROLINE ADDERSON

illustrated by HELEN FLOOK

ORCA BOOK PUBLISHERS

Library and Archives Canada Cataloguing in Publication

Adderson, Caroline, 1963-
I, Bruno / written by Caroline Adderson ; illustrated by Helen Flook.
(Orca echoes)

ISBN 978-1-55143-501-5

I. Flook, Helen II. Title. III. Series.
PS8551.D3267I17 2007   jC813'.54   C2007-903958-8

First published in the United States, 2007
Library of Congress Control Number: 2007930906

Summary: A series of stories for young readers about a boy with a strong personality
and a rich imagination.

Orca Book Publishers gratefully acknowledges the support for its publishing
programs provided by the following agencies: the Government of Canada
through the Canada Book Fund and the Canada Council for the Arts,
and the Province of British Columbia through the BC Arts Council
and the Book Publishing Tax Credit.

*Orca Book Publishers is dedicated to preserving the environment and
has printed this book on Forest Stewardship Council® certified paper.*

Cover artwork and interior illustrations by Helen Flook
Author photo by Caroline Adderson (self-taken)

ORCA BOOK PUBLISHERS   ORCA BOOK PUBLISHERS
PO Box 5626, Stn. B   PO Box 468
Victoria, BC Canada   Custer, WA USA
v8R 6s4   98240-0468

www.orcabook.com
Printed and bound in Canada.

17 16 15 14 • 6 5 4 3

For Patrick, boy inspiration.

Contents

 Bruno Eats the Rainbow ... 1

 Bruno, the Queen ... 9

Bruno, Dragonslayer ... 18

 Bruno, Hard at Work ... 26

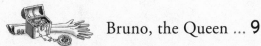 Bruno Speaks Car ... 35

I, Bruno ... 44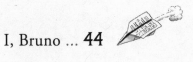

Bruno Eats the Rainbow

In the morning it was raining. Bruno wore his raincoat and new rubber boots to school. Mom carried an umbrella. The wind kept turning it inside out.

"Uh-oh," Bruno said each time. "Your under-umbrella is showing!"

It rained all through recess. It rained all through lunch. But when Bruno walked out of school at the end of the day, the sun was shining. Not only that. A huge rainbow filled half the sky.

Mom was waiting for him. She asked, "Should we go home? Or should we walk to the end of the rainbow and find the pot of gold?"

"I would walk to the end of the rainbow," said Bruno, "if there was a pot of macaroni there." He was hungry. He couldn't eat his sandwich at lunch. Someone had snuck lettuce into it.

Mom said, "Then let's walk home. That's where the macaroni is."

On the way, they passed a lot of flowers. Yellow flowers. Red flowers. Purple flowers. Orange flowers. A rainbow of flowers. Mom kept stopping to look at them. "I love spring," she said. "It's such a colorful time of year."

Bruno's empty stomach said, "Let's get a move on, please."

At home, Bruno gobbled up Mom's macaroni. It tasted so good! Then he saw something in the bottom of the bowl. Something was hiding in the cheese. "Ah!" he screamed. "There's green in my macaroni!"

"It's just zucchini," Mom said. "Just a tiny little bit."

"It's green!" Bruno put down his spoon. He wasn't hungry anymore.

But by dinner he was starving again. He stood in the kitchen door. "Is it safe to come in?" he asked.

"What do you mean?" Dad asked.

"Is there any green on my plate?"

"No," Mom said, "the coast is clear."

Bruno sat down at the table with his parents.

"What's the matter with green?" Dad asked. "Grass is green. Frogs are green."

"Your new rubber boots are green," Mom said.

"Don't you like grass and frogs?" Dad asked.

"Don't you like your new rubber boots?" Mom asked.

"I do like grass and frogs and my new boots," Bruno told them. "But I don't want to eat them. I never want to eat green again."

"Okay," Dad said. "I got it. No green. Now eat your un-green supper."

The next morning at breakfast, Dad said to Bruno, "What color will you eat today?"

Bruno named his favorite color: brown. His name, Bruno, meant brown. Mom and Dad had named him Bruno because he was born with lots and lots of brown hair sticking out all over his head.

"Brown it is," Dad said. He made Bruno hot chocolate and toast with peanut butter. "And what color should I put in your lunch?" Dad asked.

Bruno thought about it. "Orange," he said.

Dad filled Bruno's lunch kit. He put in an orange. He put in carrot sticks. He put in macaroni with orange cheese. And he put in a box of mango juice for Bruno to wash down his orange lunch.

That night, Bruno asked for a white dinner. Mom gave him a glass of milk, a potato and two hard-boiled eggs. He wouldn't eat the yolks.

"They're yellow," Bruno said.

The next day was Saturday. Bruno got to sleep late. He dreamed he was floating on his back in a huge swimming pool. Above him, the sky was the same color as the water.

When he woke up, he was hungry for blue.

Mom said, "Hmm. How about pancakes? I think there are some blueberries in the freezer."

When breakfast was ready, Bruno looked at the pancakes on his plate. "I see more brown than blue," he said.

Mom opened a new bottle of blueberry syrup. She poured it over the pancakes.

Then she took a box out of the cupboard. Inside the box were three very small bottles. One was red, one was blue and one was yellow.

"What are those?" Bruno asked.

"Food coloring." She put a drop of blue in Bruno's milk. She stirred it with a spoon. The milk looked like a glass of sky with the cloud mixed in.

That weekend Bruno also ate yellow: scrambled eggs, a banana, lemonade. He ate purple: stir-fried cabbage, blackberry yogurt, grape juice. He ate red: strawberries, baked beans with ketchup, cranberry cocktail. He ate pink: grapefruit, ham, cake.

On Sunday night, Mom said, "Bruno, now you have eaten every color but one."

"What color?" Bruno asked.

"Watch."

Mom brought two of the little bottles to the dinner table. She added a drop of blue to his milk.

"I already ate blue," Bruno said.

"I know. Watch this." She added a drop from the yellow bottle. When she stirred, Bruno saw green.

"No!" Bruno cried. "No green!"

Dad brought dinner to the table: pesto pizza, salad and a bowl of green grapes. Two of these things Bruno liked. He got an idea.

"There's one more color I haven't eaten," he said. "Black!"

He put his napkin over his head. To be on the safe side, he closed his eyes too. A lot of dinner fell into his lap. But what got into his mouth didn't taste green. It tasted great.

Bruno, the Queen

Bruno's Nana lived in an apartment near Bruno's house. Bruno liked to visit her. She had an elevator to ride up and down. Also, she never made him eat green. She didn't like eating green herself. "Down with green!" she always said. Her favorite dinner was sausages and mashed potatoes. She called them "bangers and mash." Nana served Bruno's bangers and mash on a special plate with a picture of the Queen of England on it.

Nana had lots of old clothes in a trunk. Bruno liked the smell of the old clothes. He liked to lie in the trunk with the lid closed. He would call, "Nana! Nana!" When she came looking for him, he would

throw open the lid and jump out. Every time, Nana screamed. Then she let him dress up in the clothes.

Sometimes Bruno slept over at Nana's. Before bed, she would tell him stories about when she was young and beautiful. When she was young and beautiful, she lived in England. She had seen the Queen in person.

"She's much nicer in person than on TV," Nana said one night. "She's wonderful! She's the most important person in the world!"

"If she's the most important person in the world," Bruno asked, "why do people eat sausages off her face?"

Nana laughed.

The Queen wasn't just the Queen of England, Nana told him. She was Queen of many, many countries. Bruno had not even heard of some of the countries.

The next day, Bruno went home. That night he went to sleep in his own bed. He wondered what it would be like to be the Queen. When he woke up in the morning, he was the Queen.

He went into the kitchen for breakfast. "I'm the Queen today," he told Mom.

"We have to go to the library this morning," Mom said. "Can't you be the Queen when we get back?"

"I'm the Queen now," Bruno said. "What do you think the Queen eats for breakfast?"

"Toast and peanut butter," Mom said.

"Then that's what I'll have," Bruno said. He added, "Thank you very much!" Nana said the Queen had very good manners.

Mom was happy. She said, "I like this Queen talk!"

After breakfast, Bruno put on his Bruno clothes. Then he put on his Queen clothes. He put on the golden skirt that used to be Mom's. He put on a red velvet cape. Mom had sewn the cape for him to be the King. But Bruno wasn't the King today. He was the Queen. He was the most important person in the world. He put on all his necklaces. He put on his crown. Lastly, he put on the long white gloves that Nana used to wear when she was young and beautiful. They went up to Bruno's shoulders and looked very royal.

"I'm ready," the Queen told Mom.

"Are you sure you want to go out like that?" Mom asked.

"Yes! I'm the Queen!"

"All right. But someone might say something to you."

"What?"

"They might say, 'If you're a boy, why are you wearing a dress?'"

"It's a skirt," the Queen said. "And I'm not a boy. I'm the Queen."

They left the house with the library books in a bag. "Wait!" the Queen cried. Mom had to unlock the door so she could run back in for her scepter.

On the way to the library, the Queen walked a little bit ahead. After all, she was the most important person in the world. A block from home, they met a woman. She stopped and bowed. Mom was right. She did say something. "Your Majesty," she said, "will you bless me with your scepter?"

The Queen smiled. She touched the woman's shoulder with the scepter.

"Thank you, your Majesty!"

"You're welcome," the Queen said.

At the next corner an old man was waiting to cross the street. He had two little dogs on leashes. "Don't you look nice!" he told the Queen. The little dogs wagged their tails so hard their bottoms wiggled.

Closer to the library, a jogger passed by. "What a wonderful costume!" she called.

"It's not a costume!" the Queen shouted back.

"Where's the party?" someone asked at the library door.

Mom said, "Life's a party."

The Queen took the books out of the bag. She slid them across the counter. Then Mom and the Queen went to get more books. "I want a book about me," the Queen said, "so I can remember the names of all my countries."

They found a good book about the Queen. They also found a good book about snakes and one about making models out of toothpicks.

The Queen gave her library card to the librarian. The librarian said, "My goodness! This card belongs to a princess!"

"That's not the right card," the Queen told Mom.

"Doesn't it say Queen?" Mom asked.

The librarian put on her glasses. "Oh, yes. It does. I'm sorry, your Majesty."

The Queen said, "I forgive you."

They turned to leave. Then, right there in the middle of the library, the Queen began to undress.

"What are you doing?" Mom asked.

"I'm tired of being the Queen," the Queen said.

He wanted to get home and make an airport out of toothpicks.

Mom nodded. She put the skirt, the crown and the gloves in the bag with the books. The Queen took off his necklaces. He handed them to Mom. He took off the cape.

"And I was wrong," Mom said. "Everyone was very nice."

The Queen stepped out of his skirt. Bruno said, "Of course they were nice. Wouldn't you be nice if you met the Queen?"

Then Bruno walked home with Mom—Bruno himself, the person he most liked to be.

Bruno, Dragonslayer

Bruno and his mom and dad lived on a perfect street. They could walk to the park. They could walk to the library. They could walk to school.

Across the street was the fire hall. The firefighters all knew Bruno's name. If Bruno was in the yard, they would talk to him on the fire truck's speaker. "Hello, Bruno! How are you today?"

Mom liked living close to the fire hall. It made her feel safe. The firefighters were nice. The neighbors were nice. The gardens were nice.

"What a perfect street," she said.

The park was three blocks away. It had a playground and lots of trees. Bruno liked the trees

better than the playground. The climbing was better.

One tree in the park was so big it seemed like a castle. The ground around it was the dungeon. The knights lived in the middle branches. A princess was supposed to live at the top, in the turret. "Who wants to be a princess?" Bruno would shout. Lots of girls would come running. But when they saw how high the turret was, they went back to the swings. So Sir Bruno and the other knights hung around in the branches, princess-less.

Sir Bruno's dad sat on a park bench, talking on his phone. When it was time to go home, he made the sound of a trumpet with his hands.

One day when they were walking home from the park, Bruno found a perfect stick. It was as long as his arm and very straight. He didn't want to waste it.

"This is my sword," Sir Bruno said.

They walked a little farther. Sir Bruno waved his sword while they walked. He stabbed the air.

If only a knight would come around the corner! Sir Bruno was so busy he almost didn't notice the dragon waiting by the curb. Dad didn't notice because his phone rang.

The dragon was bright red, except for the blue top of its head. It had two bulgy eyes and a round snout. One square tooth stuck out. Sir Bruno was sorry it only came up to his waist. But a knight couldn't be too picky. There weren't a lot of dragons around. This one seemed to be sleeping. Sir Bruno attacked. "One two, one two!" he shouted, slashing with the sword. The dragon was strong. It seemed to be made of iron. Disaster! Sir Bruno's sword broke in half! Luckily, the dragon was already dead.

Dad caught up. "Why are you lying on the sidewalk?" he asked.

"I'm wounded," Sir Bruno said.

Dad knelt beside him. "Where?"

Sir Bruno showed him. Dad's kiss healed him. They walked on.

Halfway down the next block, Sir Bruno and Dad saw another dragon. "What kind of street are we living on?" Dad said. "This is crazy!"

"Quick!" Bruno shouted. "A sword!"

Dad picked a stick off the ground. Sir Bruno charged and killed the dragon.

"That was a close one, son," Dad said. He patted Sir Bruno on the back.

The very next block they saw a third dragon! Bruno threw the stick down. "Forget it!" he said. Slaying dragons was too much work!

"What?" Dad asked. "You're not going to protect me?" He stepped quickly behind Bruno.

"Your phone! Your phone!" Bruno shouted. "Call nine-one-one!"

Just then a white truck drove up. A man wearing coveralls got out. All he had for a weapon was a wrench. He grabbed the dragon by the tooth. The dragon opened its mouth to roar. Instead of fire, water gushed out.

"Will you look at that?" Dad said.

"I don't think those were very dangerous dragons," Bruno said. He felt bad about the two he had killed.

At dinner that night, Bruno and Dad told Mom everything.

"Dragons? On our perfect street?" She shivered.

After school the next day, Bruno wanted to go back to the park. He wanted to be Sir Bruno again. Mom didn't want to go. "With dragons all along the way?" she said.

"Don't worry," Bruno told her. "I'll protect you."

On the way to the park they passed all three dragons. Bruno hadn't killed them after all! They were alive, and they were tame! A man came by with a dog. Bruno stepped in front of Mom to protect her. The dog tried to lift its leg on the dragon. Bruno protected the dragon too. "There's a tree right there!" he told the dog.

Bruno and Mom patted the dragon's blue head. "See?" he said. "It won't bite."

It was nice to live on a perfect street again.

Bruno, Hard at Work

After school Bruno went over to Ravi's house. Ravi was his best friend. He was his best friend and he was his friend with the best toys. Ravi had a remote-controlled robot-dog. He had a two-car racetrack. He even had a real piano.

"Ravi, you have the best toys," Bruno told him.

"You have the best toys," Ravi told Bruno.

"No, you do!"

"You do!" Ravi said.

"What are you talking about?" Bruno said. "This is the best racetrack. Look how fast the cars go around."

"It makes me carsick," Ravi said. "You've got a real wizard den."

"It's not really a wizard den," Bruno said. "It's the box the fridge came in. You've got a remote-controlled robot-dog."

Ravi said, "Its batteries are always dead. You've got a real dog."

"I do not!" Bruno said. "But you've really got a real piano!"

"Take it," Ravi said. "Then I won't have to practise."

Ravi's mother came in the room. "Are you boys getting along?" she said.

Ravi and Bruno said, "Yes!"

"Did you show Bruno your new model?" Ravi's mother asked.

Ravi jumped up. "Come on, Bruno!"

They ran to the dining room. The model was on the table. It was an army airplane. "It has three hundred and sixty-one pieces," Ravi told Bruno. "I made it with my mom."

"This is the best model airplane," Bruno said.

Ravi said, "You're right about that."

The doorbell rang. It was Bruno's mom. Bruno showed her the model airplane. "How long till my birthday?" he asked.

"A long time," Mom said.

"How long till Christmas?"

"Longer," Mom said.

At dinner that night, Bruno asked his parents, "Do you think if all my teeth fall out at once, the Tooth Fairy will put a model airplane under my pillow?"

"No," Dad said, "she'll put a set of false teeth. What's going on?"

Bruno told him about the model. Dad said, "There must be an easier way to earn some money."

"Why don't you sell the toys you don't play with anymore?" Mom said.

Bruno thought this was a good idea. After dinner he went to his room and looked at his toys. He decided to make two piles. One pile would be for the toys he would sell. The other pile would be for the toys he would keep. He picked up a car. One of its wheels was missing because Bruno had played with it so much. He played with it so much because he loved it. He put it in the Keep Pile.

Next he picked up a stuffed pig from his bed. He looked at its sad pink face. Bruno put the pig in the Keep Pile too.

An hour later, he came out of his room and said, "There must be an easier way to earn some money."

Mom said, "How about a lemonade stand?"

"Will I have to make the lemonade?" Bruno asked.

"Of course," Mom said.

"That's too much work."

"Working is a lot of work," Dad said.

Bruno looked out the window. Across the street at the fire hall, the firefighters were standing around chatting. Bruno got an idea. "I'm going to have a stand. But I'm going to sell something else."

After school the next day, Bruno set up a table in the front yard. He put a jar on the table and waited for somebody to come by. For a long time, nobody did. Then a firefighter came over.

"What are you doing, Bruno?" she asked.

"I'm selling chats," he said.

"How much?" asked the firefighter.

Bruno said, "Pay what you can."

"Are you saving up to buy something?"

Bruno told her all about the model. When he was finished, she put a dollar in the jar.

Soon another firefighter came over. He told Bruno how much he loved making models when he was a boy. After they finished talking, he put two dollars in the jar. Bruno gave him a dollar in change.

"No, that was a two-dollar chat for sure."

"But you did most of the talking," Bruno told him.

The firefighter said, "Sometimes listening is a lot of work."

By the time Bruno's mom called Bruno in for dinner, he had five dollars. The next day he earned six dollars having chats with the firefighters. He had a chat about baseball. He had a chat about why pajamas don't have pockets. And he had a chat about the best way to drink hot chocolate.

"Marshmallows?" the firefighter asked Bruno.

"Three!" Bruno said.

In just three days he had earned enough to buy the model.

But that day the firefighters put a sign up at the fire hall: *Food Drive Today*.

"Why are they driving food around?" Bruno asked his mom.

"They're not. They're collecting food and money for people who don't have enough to eat."

"Do we have any marshmallows?" Bruno asked.

Mom got two cans of soup out of the cupboard. "We'll drop this off on the way to school."

They walked across the street to the fire hall. Mom put the cans in the collection box. Bruno put the money from his chats in the box. "Why did you do that?" Mom asked.

"It would be worse not to have marshmallows for your hot chocolate than not to have a model," Bruno told her.

When Bruno got home from school that day, the model airplane was waiting for him on the table.

"Did you buy it for me?" Bruno asked.

"Yes," Mom said.

"Thank you!" cried Bruno. He opened the box: 361 pieces! "Uh-oh," he said. "This looks like a lot of work."

Bruno Speaks Car

Bruno was working on his pencil-shavings collection. He sharpened all his pencil crayons into a box. Then he drew a lot of pictures, so he could make more shavings.

Dad came in the bedroom. "Don't you understand English?" he asked.

This was what he always said when Bruno didn't do what he was told.

"I understand it," Bruno answered. "But sometimes I don't hear it."

"Put on your pajamas! Brush your teeth! Go to the bathroom! Get to bed!"

Bruno said, "I hear you now."

Weeeee eeee!!

He did all the things Dad asked. Mom and Dad kissed him good night. Dad turned out the light. Bruno lay in the dark, listening. He could hear Mom and Dad talking in the other room, but he couldn't understand what they were saying. Their voices were too quiet. He remembered the man who lived in his Nana's apartment building. He didn't speak English. He only spoke Chinese. When Nana met him in the hall, she always yelled, "Hello, Mr. Chin!" Mr. Chin

36

could hear Nana, but he couldn't understand her. So Nana yelled even louder, "How are you today?" Mr. Chin couldn't even understand her when she yelled.

Bruno was just about asleep. Across the street, a fire truck left the fire hall. "Weeeeeee!!!" the siren screamed. Bruno's bed shook as the truck went by. Even after it had passed, things didn't quiet down.

He heard, "Nee na! Nee na! Nee na!"

He heard, "OoooOOO! OoooOOO! OoooOOO!"

Bruno sat up. "What's all that racket?"

Dad came in to find out what he was shouting about. "I can't sleep," Bruno told him. "It's too noisy."

Dad closed the window. "Those are car alarms," he said. "The fire truck set them off."

"Nee na! Nee na! Nee na!" one car said.

"OoooOOO! OoooOOO! OoooOOO!" the other said.

"What are they talking about?" Bruno asked.

"I don't know," Dad said. "I don't speak Car." He kissed Bruno good night again.

37

Bruno could still hear the cars through the closed window. He tried to figure out what they were saying. The cars were probably talking about the fire truck. They were mad about being woken up. Who did that fire truck think he was? Those cars had a lot of driving to do the next day! Finally, one of the cars stopped talking, but the other went on and on. It was probably thirsty for a drink of gas.

The next day was Saturday. Bruno and Mom got in the car to go to swimming lessons. Bruno asked Mom to make the car talk. She honked the horn. "No," Bruno said, "not like that. Like this: Nee na! Nee na! OoooOOO!"

Mom pressed a button on the key. The car said, "Wa wa wa wa!"

Bruno was very surprised. "Our car speaks a different language from the other cars on our street."

"Our car is from Sweden," Mom said.

"Where are the other cars from?"

"Some are made in Canada. Some are made in Japan. Some are made in the USA."

They drove to the pool. When Bruno got out of the car, he hugged the door and said, "Wa wa wa!" He was trying to say, "Thanks for the ride, Car!"

Mom pressed the button on the key. The car answered, "Wa wa wa wa!" Bruno thought it was saying, "See you later, Bruno. Have a terrific swim."

Bruno's friend Ravi took swimming lessons too. When Ravi drove up, Bruno ran to Ravi's car. "Wa wa wa," he said. The car didn't answer. It couldn't understand Bruno.

"I was speaking Swedish Car," Bruno told Ravi.

After swimming, the parking lot was full. None of the cars was talking. The drive to the pool had made them tired. They were napping.

Mom told Bruno to watch out for cars backing out. He walked past a silver car. Its lights began to flash. It said, "You are too close! Stand back! You are too close! Stand back!"

Bruno could understand what it was saying! It spoke English! Mom laughed and laughed.

Bruno practised speaking Car all weekend. He spoke so much Car he started to forget how to speak English.

When Dad asked, "What do you want for lunch, Bruno?", Bruno answered, "Weeeeee!"

When Mom asked, "Has anyone seen my glasses?", Bruno answered, "Nee na! Nee na! Nee na!"

On Sunday, he went to visit Nana with his parents. Nana gave Bruno a big hug. "How's my best boy?" she asked.

"OoooOOO!" Bruno said.

Nana looked surprised.

"Bruno speaks Car now," Mom and Dad explained.

For dinner, Nana made bangers and mash. Mom and Dad put out a salad. Bruno saw it. "You are too close! Stand back! Stand back!" he said.

Later Nana came down in the elevator with them to say good-bye. Halfway down, the elevator stopped. The door opened. Mr. Chin stepped inside.

"Hello, Mr. Chin!!!!" Nana yelled. "How are you, Mr. Chin?!!!"

Mr. Chin pointed at Bruno. He smiled and said, "Ni how."

Bruno said, "Weeeeee!"

Mr. Chin laughed and said, "Hern how!"

"Wa wa wa wa!" Bruno told him.

Mr. Chin nodded. He pretended to be driving.

Nana asked, "What's he saying, Bruno?"

"He says you're a nice lady, but you yell a lot."

Everybody laughed. Then the elevator opened and they all got out.

"Nee na! Nee na!" Bruno said.

"Bye-bye," Mr. Chin said, waving. "Honk! Honk!"

I, Bruno

Bruno folded his report card into a paper airplane. He flew it home from school.

"That's a great plane," Mom told him.

"Yes," Bruno said. "Report cards fly very well."

"What?" Mom picked the report card off the sidewalk where it had crashed. She unfolded it and read it. "Well," she said, "there's good news and there's bad news."

"What's the good news?" Bruno asked.

"You're doing well in school."

"What's the bad news?"

"Your airplane is grounded."

When they got home, Mom ironed the report card.

The next week, Mom did more ironing. This was very strange. She hated ironing. Dad hated ironing. Bruno wasn't allowed to iron. They were a very wrinkly family.

"What's going on?" Bruno asked her. "What's all this ironing about?"

"It's about the parent-teacher meeting we have tonight with Ms. Allen," Mom said.

"Why do you need to have a meeting with Ms. Allen?" Bruno asked.

"To talk about your report card."

"But you already ironed it!" Bruno said.

"And now I'm ironing us," she said. "I don't want Ms. Allen to know how wrinkly we are."

After supper, Mom and Dad and Bruno put on their ironed shirts. They walked to the school. Ms. Allen welcomed them. She asked Bruno to show his parents his desk. She asked him to show his artwork. Then they all sat down and talked about Bruno.

"Bruno is a wonderful child," Ms. Allen said. "He is smart. He is funny. He sings very loudly."

Bruno yawned.

"I have only one problem with Bruno," Ms. Allen said.

Bruno perked up. A boy wants to be a problem sometimes.

"Bruno always forgets to write his name on his work," Ms. Allen said.

"Don't worry, Ms. Allen," Mom and Dad told her. "We'll work on that."

The next day after school they started to work on Bruno's problem. Mom put a paper and pencil on the table in front of Bruno. She said he had to write his name.

"Why?" Bruno asked.

"Because Ms. Allen says you always forget to write your name on your work."

"I don't forget," Bruno said. "By the time I've finished writing all the answers, I'm too tired."

"That's no excuse," Mom said.

"Why can't she write it?" Bruno asked.

"There are too many kids for her to write everybody's name." She gave him the pencil. "What's the first letter?"

"X," Bruno said. "Z. W."

"Write B," Mom said. "Show me."

Bruno wrote a *B*. "There," Bruno said. "Now let's go to the park."

"We're not finished," Mom said.

"B is enough," Bruno said. "Ms. Allen will know B is for Bruno."

"Aren't there any other kids in the class whose names begin with B?"

"No," Bruno said.

"What if a girl named Belinda joined the class? Or what if a boy named Bartholomew did?"

"Will they be nice?" Bruno asked.

"Who?"

"Belinda and Bartholomew."

"They are two of the nicest kids ever," Mom said. "Now let's write R."

Bruno wrote *R*. He wrote *U*. He wrote *N*. Then he said his hand was tired. "I can't write any more."

"There's only one more letter," Mom said.

"I'll write it tomorrow."

"One more letter."

"My name is too long," Bruno complained. "Why did you give me such a long name?"

"Think of poor Bartholomew," Mom said. "You only have five letters in your name. Bartholomew has eleven."

"Bartholomew has to go straight to bed after he writes his name," Bruno said.

Bruno wrote *O* like Mom wanted. His BRUNO looked good, but he wasn't happy. "I want a different name," he said.

"What name?" Mom asked.

"A short name. A name without so many letters. A name that won't make me so tired."

The next day after school, Mom tried to get Bruno to practise writing his name again. "I'll write it by myself," Bruno said. "Go away. I'll call you when I'm done."

Mom went away. Bruno got a drink of milk from the fridge. Then he called Mom back.

"There's nothing written here," Mom said.

"There is," Bruno said. He pretended to read BRUNO on the page. "It's invisible."

"I should have called you Sam," Mom said. "I wanted to, but Dad liked Bruno better."

"S-A-M," Bruno said. "Three letters. Too many."

"How about Ed?" Mom said.

"E-D. Two letters. That's better," Ed said.

Ed and Mom practised writing ED. It didn't take very long. Ed was happy. They went to the park.

Ed had a lot of fun that day. But the other knights kept calling Sir Ed, Sir Bruno, by mistake. Mom kept calling Ed, Bruno, too. She called, "Bruno! Time to go!"

"Who's Bruno?" Ed called back.

When Mom remembered to call Ed, Ed, Ed sometimes didn't answer. When Dad got home, he called Ed, Bruno, again. It was very confusing.

At bedtime Bruno said he didn't like being Ed anymore. "Isn't there another short name for me?"

"There's Al," Dad said. "No, here's a better one. Me."

Bruno was excited. "I can be Me and Bruno!"

Then Bruno remembered a shorter name, the shortest name of all.

A few minutes later Mom came in to say good night too. "Good night, Bruno."

"I'm not Bruno."

"Right. Good night, Ed."

"Wrong again!"

"Oh, right. You're Me now."

"You're Me," Bruno said.

"Then who are you?"

Bruno said, "I am I."

He wrote it at school the next day for Ms. Allen. It was so easy he filled the whole top of the page with himself. And he wasn't even tired.

Caroline Adderson writes for both children and adults and has won two Ethel Wilson Fiction Prizes, three CBC Literary Awards, as well as the 2006 Marion Engel Award given annually to an outstanding female writer in mid-career. Her numerous nominations include the Scotiabank Giller Prize longlist, the Governor General's Literary Award, the Rogers' Trust Fiction Prize and the Commonwealth Writers' Prize. Most recently, Caroline was the Vancouver Public Library's 2008 Writer-in-Residence. Caroline and her family live in Vancouver, British Columbia.